# AIRPLANES of the FUTURE

# AIRPLANES
## of the
# FUTURE

*Don Berliner*

Lerner Publications Company
Minneapolis

**Page 1: An artist's conception of a fighter plane for the year 2001 and beyond**

**Page 2: A 21st-century _Trans-Atmospheric Vehicle_ (see page 35)**

**Page 5: A delta-winged hypersonic transport with a ramjet engine (see page 33)**

**Page 6: The Grumman _X-29_ research fighter plane (see page 46)**

Copyright © 1987 by Lerner Publications Company

Library of Congress Cataloging-in-Publication Data

Berliner, Don.
    Airplanes of the future.

    Includes index.
    Summary: Describes some of the many planes being
designed today as designers and engineers experiment
with new ideas, materials, fuels, and control systems
to develop planes that will fly faster, further,
higher, and more efficiently.
    1. Airplanes—Juvenile literature. [1. Airplanes]
I. Title.
TL547.B4178     1987        629.133′34        86-10660
ISBN 0-8225-1580-6 (lib. bdg.)

Manufactured in the United States of America

  2   3   4   5   6   7   8   9   10   97   96   95   94   93   92   91   90   89   88

Airplanes of the future will be so fast, so quiet, and so efficient that they will make today's airplanes seem crude and very old fashioned. They will fly from New York to Paris quicker than a 1980s plane can fly from New York to Chicago. They will take off and land so quietly that they can use downtown airports without making a disturbance. And they will be able to carry heavier loads on less fuel. Although an estimated one million airplanes have been built since the Wright brothers first plane in 1903, people believe that the next 10 or 20 years may see greater changes in airplane design than in any period of time since World War II.

# CONTENTS

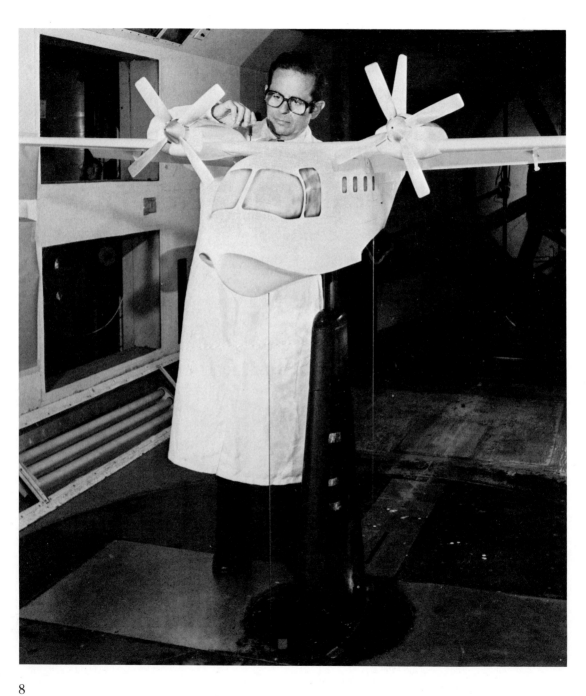

# INTRODUCTION

Right now, thousands of men and women are designing airplanes that won't fly for 10 or 25 or even 100 years. They study the best of the old planes as well as the very latest ideas in engines, materials, and airplane design. Then they look far into the future to try to find better ways of building airplanes for tomorrow. All the while, they know they are competing with people at other companies who are designing planes to achieve the same goals.

Successful designers are people with imagination who can quickly adapt to the challenge of using the newest construction materials and designs. They know that even after more than 80 years of airplane building, there are still many improvements to be made and new ideas to be tried. These designers want to create airplanes that will fly faster, farther, and higher. The new planes must also carry larger payloads while using less fuel and be safer, quieter, and less expensive to build and to operate. This book describes some of these innovative designs.

Left: A technician makes an adjustment on a model of a future amphibious plane (a plane that can operate from both land and water).

# CREATING A NEW AIRPLANE

It takes many years to create a new airplane. First, the aviation needs of the future must be determined and ways to meet them thought out. Once all of the ideas have been sorted through and the best ones decided on, a new airplane is built. Then the plane has to be tested, redesigned, and re-tested until it works.

The first step in designing a new airplane is coming up with an idea that won't be out of date by the time the plane is ready to be produced. Then aviation engineers must study the idea to see if it makes sense. Will the plane really work? Or is it just another neat scheme that can't be turned into a working model?

Once the engineers agree that they have developed a workable idea, other people must figure out if it is practical to build the airplane and if anyone will want to buy it. Will the plane be too expensive to build and to operate? Will it use too much fuel? Will it be able to fly from existing airports or will new, larger airports be needed? Finally, will the plane be better than those being built by rival companies?

These questions are very difficult to answer, and few can be answered with certainty in the early stages of a plane's development. Companies that hope to build better airplanes will often have to guess at the answers and then take some big risks. If a company guesses wrong, it could spend a great deal of money to produce an airplane that no one will buy. But if it guesses right, it will sell a lot of airplanes.

Left: A modern computer of today is used to create an airplane for tomorrow.

A full-sized prototype of the Grumman *X-29* (see pages 6 and 46) is given careful scrutiny.

# Materials

After the company's engineers and executives agree on the new design, a *prototype* of the airplane must be built. This is the first version of the plane, and it will be used only for testing. If the prototype is very different from anything the company had built before, building it could take several years.

During the early years of aviation, airplanes were built from bamboo and pine and were covered with cloth. Later, many planes were made of welded steel tubing and plywood and covered with wood and cloth. Then came modern-day aluminum planes, which were very strong and light.

Today, there are new ways of building airplanes called *composite construction.* This mixing or bonding of two or more different kinds of materials with a special adhesive makes it possible to mold planes in unusual and wonderful new shapes. As a result, engineers are free to design planes that would have been too expensive and too difficult to build from aluminum or wood. These new shapes also do a much better job of guiding the flow of air around the plane, allowing it to fly better on less gasoline or jet fuel.

The first composite airplanes were built from blocks of plastic foam (like styrofoam) that were carved and sanded and then covered with fiberglass cloth and epoxy resin. These airplanes were much stronger and lighter than those built from metal, wood, and cloth, and they could fly faster and further on less fuel.

The next composite airplanes were built of some very expensive materials like carbon fibers and graphite fibers. Airplanes from such materials were even stronger and lighter than foam-and-fiberglass planes. In the future, even better composite materials will certainly be developed.

Along with their advanced shapes and materials, some airplanes of the future may use new types of engines, and many will use new kinds of fuels. Others may have new types of control systems, and some may be different in ways that no one can yet imagine. All of them, however, will be exciting to see and to fly.

# Test Flying

When the prototype has been completed, it will be test-flown by the company's best test pilot. The pilot must know enough about testing new airplanes to be able to tell if it is as good as it is supposed to be. In the past, the first few test flights of a new airplane were dangerous, and many fine test pilots crashed and lost their lives.

Today, however, computers can predict almost exactly how a new airplane will fly, which is a much safer way to test the crucial details of a design.

After each test flight, some changes are usually made in the plane. Perhaps the prototype is a little out of balance so some of its weight will have to be shifted forward or to the back (aft). Maybe one of the controls didn't work smoothly, so it will have to be adjusted. Or maybe the airplane didn't recover from a spin quickly enough, so a bigger change, such as re-designing the entire tail, will have to be made. Making these changes may take weeks, even months.

Once everyone is satisfied with the way the plane flies, it is time to think about building more of them. Several years may have now passed since the first designer started to think about creating this new airplane.

If the ideas that first went into the new design were clever enough, the plane may be put into production and be a success. And if the design was futuristic enough, the airplane may be exactly what people will be looking for when it is ready for use. Then if other aviation manufacturers haven't already done a better job of creating a similar plane, the new airplane could be an important step forward in aviation history.

Across: In a wind tunnel, a model of a future tilt-engine airplane is tested for its response to wind force. Above: A plane's capacity for reflecting radar waves is studied at an outdoor range.

# PERSONAL AIRPLANES

## 2

Most small airplanes used by people for personal business and for recreational travel haven't changed much in the past 30 years. Two-passenger planes still cruise at about 120 miles per hour (193 kilometers per hour), getting less than 20 miles (32 km) to a gallon of gasoline, and only the most expensive four-passenger personal planes fly much faster than 150 mph (240 km/h). The next 10 to 20 years, however, should see big changes in personal planes.

The main goal of designers is to develop small planes that are lighter, more streamlined, and, as a result, more fuel efficient. The new planes will be very different from the thousands of

Left: Built with one wing behind the cockpit and another near the nose, the *Quickie* home-built sportplane has been a model for future factory-built personal planes.

planes now being built by Piper, Cessna, and Beech, the largest manufacturers of personal airplanes. As with larger planes, the use of composite materials will make these new designs possible.

## The Home-Builts

Although commercial builders of personal airplanes do not reveal much about their plans for the future, they surely must be looking very carefully at the wonderful home-built designs that have revolutionized the world of light planes. The successful *tail-first* (the horizontal part of the tail is at the front of the plane) *VariEze* and *LongEz* developed by Burt Rutan and the *tandem-winged* (one wing is near the front of the plane and the other is about halfway back) *Quickie* and *Q2* have shown everyone just how much better small

17

planes can fly if they are truly modern in their design and construction.

Since they are constructed from plastic foam and fiberglass cloth, home-built planes are much lighter than factory-built aluminum planes. And because they are lighter, their wings can be smaller as they don't have to lift so much weight. Smaller wings create less wind resistance, or *drag*, so home-builts will fly faster and use less fuel.

Both tail-first and tandem-winged airplanes are also much safer to fly than airplanes with regular tails in the back.

When there is a wing or horizontal part of the tail, or *canard surface*, in front, the airplane won't stall and drop when it flies very slowly. And if it won't stall, the plane can't go into a dangerous spin, which is the cause of many small-plane accidents. The first new factory-built personal planes will incorporate some of these home-built design ideas.

A typical design for a larger private airplane of the future is the Avtek *400*, built by the Avtek Corporation. The *400* will carry from six to nine people on non-stop flights across the United States without having to stop for refueling. It

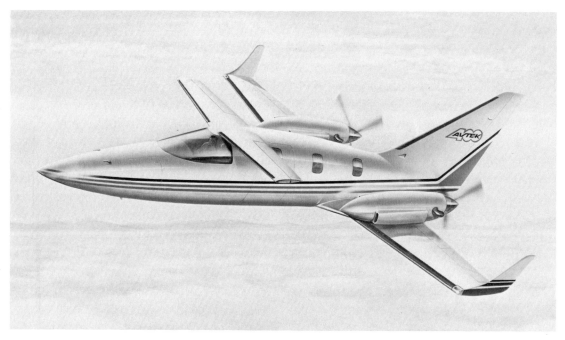

The Avtek *400*

The Rein-Flugzeugbau *Fanstar*

should weigh only half as much as any current private airplane of the same size and at high speed should get more than twice as many miles to the gallon.

The tail-first *400* has small vertical surfaces, or *winglets*, at its wingtips to help the wings operate more efficiently, and its pusher propellers face the rear so the wings won't be working in the twisting airflow created by the propellers. The plane is molded from a special

cloth that is said to be 5 times stronger than steel and 15 times stronger than aluminum.

The four-passenger *Fanstar* will not be so much a completely new shape in personal airplanes as a better way to use an engine and a propeller. A West German company, Rhein-Flugzeugbau, earlier designed and built the *Fantrainer*, a military training plane that hid its engine inside the fuselage to avoid wind resistance. The *ducted-fan* propeller, located right behind the engine, was surrounded by a *shroud*, or covering, that kept the air from spilling off the propeller tips.

The *Fanstar* will travel faster than a plane having its engine and propeller in the nose, and it will use less fuel because of its streamlined shape. Its enclosed engine and fan will also make the plane quieter for people inside and on the ground.

# Roadable Airplanes

For many years, people have been trying to develop a combination airplane and automobile that could take off and fly over traffic jams and could also be driven along the highway when the weather was not safe for flying. Although everyone thought it a great idea, no one has been able to make it work very well, and roadable airplanes, or "flying cars," have been neither very good cars nor very good airplanes. Now, however, an interesting new Boeing design for a flying car, the *Personal Electric Flivver*, could become a reality in 50 to 100 years.

When it is flying, this new ducted-fan airplane/car is really an *autogyro*, kept in the air by a helicopter-like rotor turned by air rushing over the rotor blades instead of by an engine. When the *Flivver* is used as a car, each of its

Dr. Igor Bensen's home-built autogyro, the *Gyrocopter*

wheels is powered by an individual electric motor. Both the wheels and the propeller are powered by a pair of heavy flywheels that spin around the vehicle's body. When the *Personal Flivver* is not in use, it will be plugged into an electric outlet, and its flywheels will slowly spin up to their top speed to create a store of energy. When the vehicle is moving, the energy from the flywheels will run a generator to produce electric power.

It will be many years before a *Personal Electric Flivver* will be built and tested. Or it might never happen at all. But the idea is one that just may change the way people travel.

## Supersonic Business Jets

A supersonic "dream plane" for the business world of the 21st century has been proposed by the Gates Learjet Corporation. Because Gates had already manufactured hundreds of Learjets, one of the most popular small, fast jet planes in production, their designers were already familiar with sleek, high-performance executive jets.

The proposed *Model LRXX* (see page 22) would fly at 1,200 mph (1,920 km/h), or about two times the speed of sound, which is more than twice as fast as any current executive jet. It could carry 10 passengers non-stop for 4,500 miles (7,200 km), the distance between New York City and Rome, Italy, cruising at an altitude of 60,000 feet (18,000 meters), or 11 miles. At that altitude, the air is very smooth, and there is almost no bad weather to worry about.

The *LRXX* would have a swept-forward wing, which is expected to work very well at supersonic speeds, and the winglets at its wingtips would help to control the flow of air, allowing the wing to lift a greater weight. With the wing at

the rear and a small canard surface in front, the *LRXX* could have a smaller wing and would, therefore, be a safer airplane.

## Transonic Business Jets

The Boeing Company has designed an even more unusual airplane for business use perhaps 100 years from now. Their transonic business jet would have a small, thin *variable-sweep wing* (see photo on page 31) that could be used as a helicopter rotor for takeoffs and landings at downtown *heliports*. Then when the plane was ascending, the wing could be set at right angles to the *fuselage* (body), like the straight wing on any airplane. As the jet reached its 1,000-mph (1,600-km/h) cruising speed, the wing could be swung sideways to a swept-forward position on one side of the plane and a swept-back position on the other side.

The advantage of the variable-sweep wing is having both a straight wing for use at low speeds and a swept wing, which works best at high speeds. The Boeing transonic jet's gas turbine (jet) engines would be powered by liquid hydrogen fuel, which is almost pollution-free, and the plane could fly from downtown New York City to downtown Los Angeles, California, in just three hours.

A Learjet of the future, the *Model LRXX* (see page 21)

# AIRLINERS OF THE FUTURE

## 3

Since the early 1960s, airliners have become larger and quieter, and they waste less jet fuel. Today, the cost of long trips is less than in the past because airliners carry more people, and, by using even less fuel, designs for future airliners may lower flight costs even more. Other goals, however, such as noise reduction, less air pollution, greater speed, more cargo space, and the ability to take off or land in limited space near cities are also important.

## Commuter Airliners

Smaller commuter airliners are used to carry up to 100 passengers on trips of no more than a few hundred miles. Because commuter planes fly at top speed for such a short time, speed isn't as important as being able to take off and land quickly and quietly and using as little gasoline or jet fuel as possible.

The first of the future generation of commuter airliners may actually have propellers, as did all airliners many years ago. Propellers work very well at speeds up to 400 mph (640 km/h), and new designs for propellers with numerous wide, curved blades (see page 24) are being developed to fly quietly on less fuel at 500 mph (800 km/h) or faster.

Many years from now, commuter airliners may be *tilt-winged convertiplanes*, or half airplane and half helicopter, with short wings and their engines and propellers on the wingtips. For taking off and landing at downtown heliports, these planes will tilt their engines and propellers straight up to fly like helicopters. Then when they get into the air and are moving forward, they will tilt their engines and propellers forward to fly like ordinary airplanes. Such a

Above: A commuter airliner of the future may have propellers with many wide, sharply curved blades like the ones on this proposed military cargo plane. Below: A convertiplane flies like an airplane when its propellers face forward (as shown here) and like a helicopter when its rotors are turned upwards.

tilt-winged commuter airliner could fly 100 passengers from the center of one city to the center of another city 300 miles away in less time than any regular jet airliner.

At some time in the future, commuter airliners might be powered by electricity and shaped like flying saucers. The Boeing *Electric Commuter Jet* could fly almost noiselessly, landing and taking off straight up and down from any parking lot to pick up and let off passengers like a city bus.

The Boeing electric jet would be powered by heavy flywheels that spun in opposite directions around the jet.

An artist's rendering of Boeing's *Electric Commuter Jet*, which would operate like a helicopter

On the ground, the flywheels would be gradually spun up to top speed, and, once in flight, would power an air compressor. The compressor would shoot compressed air out of the rear of the jet for forward flight and out of the bottom for vertical flight. Such a power-plant would create no pollution.

## Subsonic Airliners

Almost all of today's commercial jet airliners fly at *subsonic* speeds, or just below the speed of sound, which is about 650 mph (1,040 km/h) at high altitude. To operate efficiently, they fly as fast as possible, but not at *supersonic* speeds, or faster than sound, so as not to create sonic booms and disturb people on the ground. At that speed, they work well for flights of a few thousand miles. Subsonic airliners of the future won't fly any faster, but they will be quieter, will use less fuel, and will be able to use smaller airports.

One Boeing design for a subsonic

A futuristic McDonnell-Douglas propeller-driven subsonic airliner

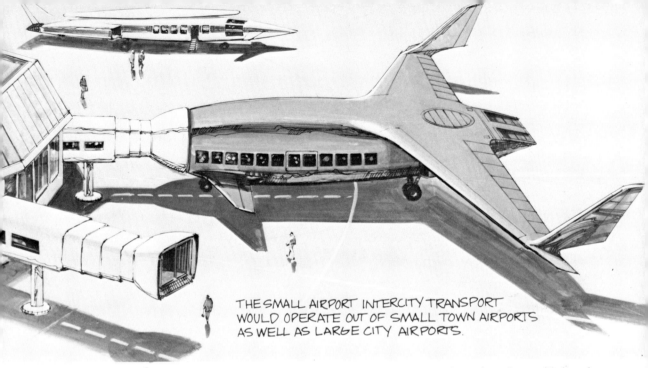

THE SMALL AIRPORT INTERCITY TRANSPORT
WOULD OPERATE OUT OF SMALL TOWN AIRPORTS
AS WELL AS LARGE CITY AIRPORTS.

Boeing's tail-first *Intercity Transport*. (Shown in the background is a swing-wing plane with its wing turned flat against the fuselage.)

airliner of the distant future has its wings in the back and its horizontal tail (canard surface) in front, just like the *VariEze* home-built two-seater. Its jet engines will burn liquid hydrogen fuel, causing almost no pollution, and it will be able to use runways as short as 1,500 feet (450 m). The airliner will fly at 500 mph (800 km/h) and will carry about 100 passengers.

In the 1930s, the first large airliners were "flying boats" that could land on water because there weren't any long, concrete runways for big landplanes. Their boat-shaped bottoms created a lot of wind resistance, however, which made them slower than landplanes.

A water-based airliner of the late 21st century would be shaped more like a landplane than a seaplane and, using an air-cushion landing gear, would be able to land on and take off from water. When the plane was close to the water, the air blowing out of its bottom and wingtips would create a cushion of air for it to ride on. Although it would be new for airplanes, such an air-cushion system has been used for many years on passenger-carrying craft called *ground-effect machines* or *hovercraft*. These craft skim a few feet above the water on a cushion of air and work much better than boats that must drag their hulls through the water.

Boeing has designed a new *amphibious* plane for use 100 or so years in the future. Its proposed *Large Amphibian* would not have to use airports with long runways but could operate from both land and water, which would be very convenient because so many of the world's major cities are on or close to oceans, lakes, or large rivers. The *Amphibian* would have an atomic fusion engine that would heat helium gas to operate the ducted-fan engines. It would be a very large craft that could carry up to 1,000 passengers and more than 300,000 pounds (135,000 kilograms) of cargo. Like current subsonic airliners, it would cruise at a speed of 600 mph (960 km/h).

The *Large Amphibian* could land and take off from both ground and water.

THE LARGE AMPHIBIAN WOULD OPERATE CITY CENTER TO CITY CENTER USING LARGE RIVERS AND HARBORS FOUND IN MOST MAJOR CITIES.

The *Concorde* was one of the first SSTs to travel faster than the speed of sound.

## Supersonic Airliners

The faster a jet flies, the better it flies. This is because the high-speed air rams into its engine intakes and is partly compressed even before it gets into the engines. Because the highly compressed air gives the plane a strong push when it leaves the engine, less engine power is needed for air compression. To date, the greatest advancement in airliners has been the development of *supersonic transports (SSTs)*. These beautiful *delta-winged* (triangular-winged) airplanes can fly at 1,300 mph (2,080 km/h)— more than twice the speed of sound— and can travel from London, England, to New York City in only three hours. Airliners flying that fast will offer passengers very short travel times, but they

The McDonnel-Douglas *Advanced Supersonic Transport* (page 31) will fly more efficiently and carry twice as many passengers as the *Concorde*.

will be expensive to build and will use a lot of fuel. They will also make a lot of noise, especially sonic booms, when flying over people's homes.

The first airliners to cruise faster than the speed of sound were the *Concorde*, jointly built by English and French companies, and the Tupolev *Tu-144*, which was built in the Soviet Union. These planes, however, used so much fuel and carried so few passengers that they were very costly to operate. The *Tu-144* was in use for only about six months in 1977 and 1978. While the 110-passenger *Concorde* has been in regular service for trans-Atlantic flights since 1976 and has performed very well at supersonic speeds, it, too, will probably not be in use much longer. Only a dozen

or so planes were built, and the last ones may be retired in the near future.

Perhaps in 10 or 20 years, there could be a new generation of SSTs that will be better designed with more modern fuel-saving engines. They will also be larger and will carry at least 200 passengers, which will allow the airlines to reduce their ticket prices.

Engineers today are trying to build supersonic airplanes that are less noisy, use less fuel, and will fly well at low speeds during landings and takeoffs. To achieve so many difficult goals, new planes will have to be shaped differently from today's *747* and *DC-10*. Instead, they may resemble the *Concorde* with delta wings and large vertical tails in back and small canard surfaces in front.

The McDonnell Douglas *Advanced Supersonic Transport* does look a lot like the *Concorde*. With a delta wing, conventional tail, and four powerful turbojet engines under the rear of the wing, it will carry more than 200 passengers. Its engines will use much less fuel than the *Concorde* Olympus engines, and a more streamlined shape will reduce the plane's wind resistance.

There are now only a few very large airports that can be used by SSTs because they need such long runways. Creating supersonic planes with a *swing wing*, however, would make it possible for them to operate from smaller airports. When the wing is moved from the swept position and locked in the straight-across position, it will provide more lift at low speeds and allow the

A NASA swing-wing supersonic airliner (page 32) positioned for high-speed flying with one wing forward and one back. The outline shows the wing positioned straight across for takeoff and flying at low speeds.

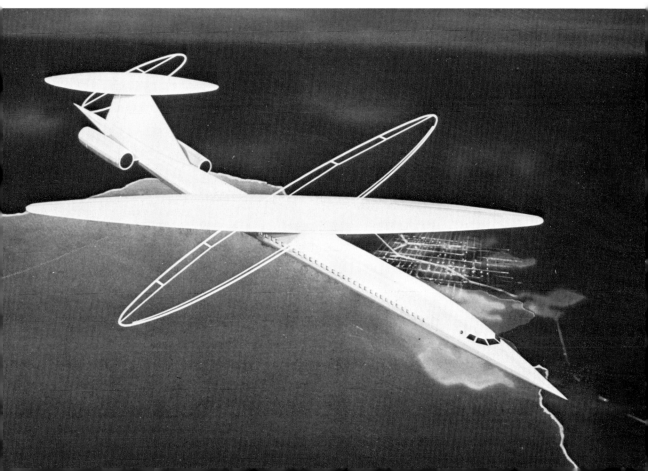

plane to take off more quickly without having to point its nose up so steeply. Then when the plane is flying at supersonic speeds, the wing will be swung into a different position, with one side swept forward and the other swept back.

A one-passenger test version of this proposed craft has been built for the National Aeronautics and Space Administration (NASA) to find out if it really works—and it does. Someday, swing-wing SSTs may be flying out of airports all over the world.

## Hypersonic Airliners

Once people get used to flying at twice the speed of sound, they will soon be thinking about *hypersonic transports (HSTs)*. (The speed of an object is considered *hypersonic* if it travels at least *five* times the speed of sound.) These amazing airplanes will fly at speeds of 3,000 to 8,000 mph (4,800-12,800 km/h) and will make it possible to travel from New York City to Tokyo, Japan, in less than two hours. They will fly as high as 100,000 to 130,000 feet (30,000-

Hypersonic transports *(HSTs)* may travel at 10 times the speed of sound. One model (top) has a delta (triangular-shaped) wing with an additional small wing near the nose, and another (below) is a variable-sweep wing craft.

HSTs will be powered by both turbojet and hydrogen-fueled ramjet engines and will cruise at nearly 4,000 miles per hour (6,400 km/h).

39,000 m), or 19 to 25 miles, where the sky will look almost black. Because a hypersonic transport is flying so fast, its passengers will experience only 5/6ths the normal pull of gravity and will feel like they are starting to go into orbit.

HSTs will have engines that use jet fuel at speeds up to 3,600 mph (5,760 km/h), which is about five times the speed of sound, or *Mach 5*. Then their *turbojet* engines will be shut down and *ramjet* engines using liquid hydrogen

fuel will be started up. The airliner would reach its top speed at such high altitudes that almost no sonic boom would be heard on the ground.

An *HST* that flies many thousands of miles in an hour would be useful for only very long trips, such as from North America to Asia. On shorter trips, it would have to begin slowing down long before it got up to its cruising speed, which would be like driving an Indianapolis 500 race car to the corner to buy a quart of milk!

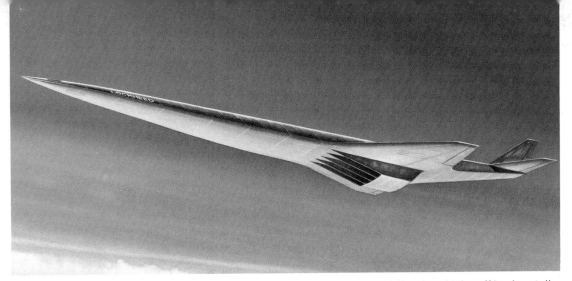

Left: The hydrogen-powered *Aerospace Plane* of the 21st century could land and take off horizontally and cruise at Mach 25, or 16,000 miles an hour (25,600 km/h) at a height of 65 miles. Above: The even faster *Trans-Atmospheric Vehicle* (*TAV*) could reach speeds of Mach 30, or 20,000 miles per hour (38,000 km/h).

Still further into the future are airliners that will fly at extreme speeds on the edge of space. These *Aerospace Planes* and *Trans-Atmospheric Vehicles* (*TAVs*) may be able to cruise at Mach 25 to Mach 30 (16,000 to 20,000 mph) from 60 to 70 miles above the Earth. So far, such craft are only ideas, but they could be in our skies within the next 20 to 30 years.

## Cargoplanes

Not all large civilian airplanes carry only passengers. Most airliners also carry freight in a hold below the passenger cabin, and some carry nothing but freight. Today, the best cargoplanes are the Boeing *747* freighter and the U.S. Air Force's Lockheed *C-5A Galaxy*.

Both are conventional, four-engine jets with huge cargo holds for carrying such large, heavy items as trucks and helicopters. In the future, airplanes designed for transporting freight will be larger than any airplane already built and will probably be shaped very differently as well.

The Lockheed Aircraft Corporation has been working on several interesting designs for future freight transports, and one of them would actually carry its cargo on the *outside* of the plane where it would be easy to load and unload. While having odd-shaped packages sticking out and causing wind resistance seems like a terrible idea, it actually wouldn't slow down the cargo liner very much because the plane would be designed to carry objects that were too large to fit inside a traditional cargo-

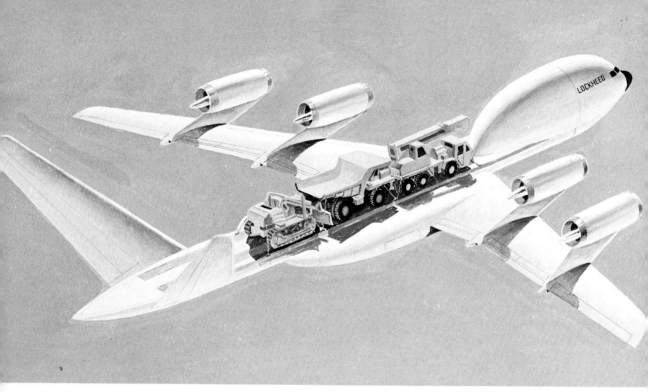

Lockheed's advanced heavy-lift cargoplane—shown here transporting construction equipment—would carry freight on the outside of the plane.

plane. The load would be tied down very carefully, and some of the cargo might be inside special freight containers that could also be fit on trains and cross-country trucks.

An idea even farther into the future is Lockheed's giant flying freighter that could carry 400,000 pounds (180,000 kg) of cargo, non-stop, to any place in the world at a speed of 500 mph (800 km/h). At that speed, the plane would reach any location within 24 hours. Powered by nuclear energy, this futuristic cargoplane would be able to fly for weeks without refueling.

To date, the most unusual idea for transporting freight is a combination airplane and *ground-effect* ship. The craft would have a very thick wing, which would also serve as its cargo hold, and the flat bottom of the wing would fly only a few feet above the water. While the craft would need much less power than if it were flying high in the sky, it should still be able to cruise along at 300 mph (480 km/h), which is much faster than any cargo ship, and it could carry 440,000 pounds (198,000 kg) of freight to any location on a large river, a lake, or an ocean.

Above: Another Lockheed cargoplane, the nuclear-powered flying freighter. Below: Still another Lockheed cargoplane could store cargo inside its wing. It could carry a heavier load than a conventional airplane and travel faster than a ship.

# MILITARY AIRCRAFT

## 4

Because the world's governments are willing to spend so much money on building military equipment, there will probably be more unusual new military airplanes than civilian planes. Just as soon as one country spends billions of dollars to build a super new airplane, a rival nation will spend even more to construct a more advanced craft.

The new military planes now being designed and tested will be built from the finest and most expensive new materials. They will have strange new shapes, and some may not look much like airplanes at all. They will have new engines and will fly further, higher, and faster than earlier models did. They

Left: Because of its shape and the materials used in its construction, the Lockheed *Advanced Tactical Fighter (ATF)* could cruise undetected at 1,000 miles per hour (1,600 km/h) or faster for long periods of time.

will carry larger loads of weapons and will be able to fly and fight in the worst possible weather, attacking ground targets and other airplanes that are too far away or too covered by thick clouds to be seen by the opposing craft.

The most important new word in military airplanes is *stealth*, and such planes will be able to fly in secret because they can barely be tracked by *radar* or other electronic devices. Radar uses electrical signals, or radar waves, that are beamed at an airplane and then bounce off, returning to a radar device located on the ground or in another airplane. The signals show the location of the airplane being tracked and where it is heading and how fast it is flying.

Ever since World War II, radar has been used to follow enemy airplanes that are too far away to be seen and to attack them before being detected. Today, that is a very difficult assignment

A U.S. Air Force fighter equipped with an advanced *Airborne Warning and Control System (AWACS)*. The rotating radome above the plane contains a radar antenna for tracking both high- and low-flying aircraft over any terrain.

because a lot of clever new ways of hiding airplanes have been invented.

All objects reflect radar waves, but some shapes and materials reflect them less than others. A small airplane, for instance, will reflect radar less than a larger plane, as will an airplane that has been built of plastics and composite materials instead of metal. An airplane with almost no flat surfaces and only curves will reflect radar waves in all directions, so most of the waves will sail off into space. And an airplane painted with special paints will absorb some of the radar waves instead of reflecting them.

It is also possible to trick an enemy's radar by equipping an airplane with very sophisticated electronic gear. Such an instrument can mix up the reflected radar waves so they will send out the wrong information to the enemy, or the frequency of the reflected radar waves may be changed so the enemy's equipment will not be able to pick them up at all. Other types of equipment are used to track an airplane in flight. Some search for heat generated by the plane's jet engines, but they can sometimes be fooled when the engine's intakes and exhaust are on top of the airplane, shielded by the wings or the tail.

# Reconnaissance Planes

Airplanes with the highest performance in speed and altitude are used for *reconnaissance*, or spying from the sky. These planes are equipped with cameras and electronic devices to find and record information about important military bases and factories. Since they usually do not carry any guns or rockets for protection against enemy attack, they have to depend on speed and stealth for survival.

Since 1965, the world's fastest and highest-flying airplane has been the U.S. Air Force Lockheed *SR-71 Blackbird*, one of the first planes designed for aerial spying. The *Blackbird* can fly as fast as 2,500 mph (4,000 km/h) and can cruise at altitudes of 100,000 feet (30,000 m), or about 19 miles, or higher. Since the *SR-71*, even faster and higher-flying spy planes have probably been designed and built, but they have been kept secret, just as the *SR-71* was kept secret for many years.

Much of the aerial reconnaissance that used to be performed by spy planes is now handled by Earth-orbiting satellites that can study any place from hundreds of miles up without any danger of being shot down. But a spy plane has an important advantage over a spy satellite in that it can be sent any place quickly for inspection. A satellite, mean-

The *SR-71 Blackbird* has held the official world air speed record (ASR) since 1976.

This Lockheed design for a future spy plane is an example of the latest in stealth technology.

while, remains in a fixed orbit and can only observe a target while passing over it, which might mean waiting for several days.

One design for a spy plane of the future comes from Lockheed, a company that knows a lot about building reconnaissance aircraft. The plane, built of special heat-resistant steels, would cruise at 3,350 mph (5,360 km/h) at an altitude of 100,000 feet (30,000 m), or about 19 miles. Its turbo-ramjet engines would function as turbojet (gas turbine) engines at low speed and then could be switched to operate as ramjets at very high speeds.

## High-Altitude Surveillance

Sometime in the 1990s, a very light, odd-looking airplane with very long wings but no pilot may take off and climb high into the sky to circle slowly while keeping an eye on the earth below. The craft may be Lockheed's solar-powered *High-Altitude Powered Platform (HAPP)*, which is designed to cruise at 70,000 feet (21,000 m) for many months at a time. The *HAPP* could be used to carry cameras and other instruments for watching how crops are growing. Or, it could be used by the U.S. Air Force to observe areas that might be trouble spots. The *HAPP* would be easier and less expensive to use than conventional airplanes with pilots or orbiting satellites because it could be positioned to fly over a limited area instead of making one pass during every orbit. And it would need no launch vehicle or any high-resolution cameras or other sensors required by high-orbiting satellites.

The large winglets at the *HAPP's* wingtips would be folded down to increase the size of the wings for better flying. On its vertical surfaces, there would be solar cells for charging batteries or fuel cells, which would produce electricity to run a motor connected to the propeller. The energy stored during the day would be used at night when there was no sun shining on the solar cells.

When the solar-powered *High Altitude Powered Platform (HAPP)* travels in sunlight, its solar cells send energy to fuel cells to operate the electric motor. During dark hours (right), the motor runs on the stored electrical power.

The McDonnell Douglas *F-15 Eagle* is widely regarded as the best fighter currently operating anywhere in the world.

# Fighter Planes

The second most advanced type of military airplane is the fighter, which must be able to defeat enemy fighters in combat. Fighters must be fast, maneuverable, and able to transport a large load of guns, rockets, or other weapons. They also need to carry a great deal of electronic equipment to help locate and to hide from enemy airplanes.

In the early 1980s, the most popular American fighter was the McDonnell Douglas *F-15 Eagle*, which flew faster than 1,600 mph (2,560 km/h) at altitudes of at least 100,000 feet (30,000 m). The Soviet Air Force *MiG-25 Foxbat* flies about as fast and as high. Since 1977, Lockheed has been flying its super-secret "stealthplane," which may be a fighter or a spy plane. Nothing is known about how fast or how high it flies, but it probably would out-perform the *F-15* and the *MiG-25*.

A two-tailed delta-wing Grumman stealthplane of the future (see page 46)

The Grumman *X-29* swept-forward wing research fighter was test flown for the first time on December 14, 1984.

Fighters of the future will certainly be stealth types, with delta wings or tail-first canards. One possible fighter design for the 1990s is Grumman's two-tailed delta. The Grumman fighter has its engine intake and exhaust concealed on top of the plane, and the exhaust can be tilted up or down for sharper maneuvering.

Another interesting design for a fighter plane of the future is Grumman's experimental *X-29 swept-forward* airplane. (An airplane with its wings slanted forward instead of back was tried during World War II, but without success.) Once

the *X-29*, with its odd-looking wings, has proven to fly better than other planes, there is a good chance that other companies will start to build similar fighters. Swept-forward planes can have a canard surface near the nose or a horizontal part on the tail in the back.

Still another Grumman design is a fighter-bomber that carries its large guided missiles on top for launching upward when the airplane is flying close to the ground. It has a conventional swept-back wing and a canard surface in front, and its engine exhaust can be tilted to help to maneuver quickly.

This Grumman fighter-bomber would carry missiles on the top of its fuselage for release at low altitudes.

The Dassault-Breguet *Aircraft Combat Experimental (ACX)*

A French design for a future fighter that may stand a better chance of actually being produced because it isn't quite as radical is Dassault-Breguet's *Aircraft Combat Experimental (ACX)*. Like so many French fighters, it has a delta wing and a canard surface up front for help in maneuvering. The *ACX,* constructed from many composite materials, would have a very advanced avionics *(avi*ation electr*onics)* system.

A lot of advanced ideas for fighters of the future have been tested on the *HiMAT,* a radio-controlled, half-size test plane. Built by Rockwell International Corporation for NASA, the *HiMAT* is launched from a Boeing B-52 bomber in flight and then controlled by a "pilot" on the ground. It has an unusual shape with a swept-back wing and winglets on its tips and a highly swept canard surface in front.

NASA's *HiMAT* half-size remote-controlled research design has been used to test many new ideas for future airplanes.

The U.S. Air Force Rockwell *B-1* bomber, which carries both conventional and nuclear weapons, was first flown in 1974.

# Bombers

Like fighters and spy planes, bombers of the future will have many stealth features. But because they are larger than fighters, they will be able to carry even more electronic equipment to escape detection by enemy radar. They will also have crew members who will operate this special equipment.

The newest U.S. bomber is Rockwell International's *B-1*. The *B-1* has variable-sweep wings for good performance at all speeds. It can fly as fast as 1,500 mph (2,400 km/h) and carry a heavy load of weapons for many thousands of miles. Bombers built in the 1990s and later will certainly fly faster and farther, however, and the first of these "stealth" bombers is expected to be built by the Northrop Corporation.

Although not much is known about Northrop's future stealth bomber, it may be a *flying wing* like the ones built by the company many years ago. Those planes had big, broad wings with no horizontal tail, and they carried their entire cargo inside the big wing.

Another Northrop design for a futuristic bomber is a canard with its wings and horizontal tail swept forward and sharply drooped down (see below). Its engines are mounted on top of the wings, which will keep an enemy's infra-red radiation detectors from locating the bomber by the heat its engines give off.

This *Advanced Strategic Bomber* designed by Northrop for the U.S. Air Force has a swept forward and drooping wing and tail for improved flying.

Another U.S. Air Force *Advanced Strategic Bomber* with winglets on the wingtips and turbojet engines on top of the wings

Among other interesting designs for future flying-wing bombers is a U.S. Air Force craft with drooping canard surfaces at the nose (above). Its engines are mounted on top of the wings, and there are winglets at the wingtips for lifting heavier loads. Another flying wing, designed by the Rockwell International Corporation, has its engines buried in the wings and no horizontal tail.

Still other futuristic bombers may have wings that change shape in flight for taking off and landing slowly and then flying at great speed. The *"X"-wing* will have one *bar,* or wing, longer than the other, and the long wing will be used for flying slowly. Then the entire wing will be rotated 90 degrees so the long wing will lie flat on the fuselage, and the shorter wing will provide the little lifting force needed for high-speed flight.

Above: This Rockwell bomber has its engines concealed in the flying wing and a laser weapon mounted on the tail. Below: The Boeing "X" wing bomber shown with its short wing functioning for high-speed flight. When flying slowly, the short wing will be rotated to lie flat against the plane's body and the longer wing will be used.

This Rockwell supersonic bomber flies at subsonic speeds with its wing straight out (above). During high-speed flights, its wing is tucked into a recess on top of the fuselage (below).

Another way to use almost the same idea is to have a straight wing for low-speed flight and then turn it 90 degrees to be flat along the top of the fuselage. Then at very high speed, the plane will get enough lift from the air passing over the fuselage to keep it in the air.

Bombers that are projected for use even further into the future—50 to 100 years away—may be powered by nuclear engines and be able to carry enough fuel for flights lasting many days. A nuclear-powered bomber would probably have to be very large and heavy so the engine could be far away from the crew and surrounded by heavy material to shield the crew from any dangerous radiation.

Two nuclear-powered U.S. Air Force bombers of the future. One (above) has a diamond-shaped wing and a canard surface in front, and the other (below) is a delta wing. Each carries a guided missile beneath its fuselage.

This Boeing Vertol "X"-wing convertiplane flies like a helicopter when its rotor, or wing, is rotating, as shown here, and like an airplane when the wing is locked in the "x" position.

This Hughes-built *NOTAR (NO TAil Rotor)* U.S. Army helicopter of the future carries missiles on the ends of its short wings.

## Rotary-Wing Aircraft

Helicopters have been popular for more than 40 years. These *rotary-wing* craft can take off straight up, land straight down, and hover motionless in mid-air. They cannot, however, fly as fast or as far as airplanes. Today, designers are working hard to develop flying machines that are part helicopter and part airplane and will be able to perform all of these maneuvers well.

While "true" helicopters of the future will probably remain an important part of aviation, like other types of aircraft, they will be very different from those we know today and will be much more streamlined to fly faster on less power. Some will be *NOTAR (NO TAil Rotor)*

craft that may use a blast of compressed air to keep the fuselage from spinning around.

In the next 10 years, convertiplanes are likely to become common. These tilt-rotor machines can fly up and down like helicoptors and straight ahead like airplanes. In the future, they may be used as commuter airliners, executive transports, and military-support craft.

One futuristic design for a convertiplane is Boeing Vertol's *"X"-wing*. Like many subsonic jets, it has a fuselage and a tail, but it also has a four-bladed rotor on top, which enables it to fly like a helicopter. When it is time for the X-wing to become an airplane and fly fast, the rotor is stopped and locked in the "X" position. Then even though

Another futuristic, highly streamlined U.S. Army helicopter from Boeing Vertol carries a great deal of electronic equipment for surveillance use.

part of the wing is swept back and part is swept forward, it works like an airplane wing.

Lots of electronic devices will be used to make helicopters and convertiplanes easier to fly in all kinds of weather, and military helicopters will be designed with stealth technology to make them harder to see and to track with radar. Composite materials will also make them lighter and stronger, and better-designed composite rotor blades will make for smoother and quieter flights.

# Anti-Submarine Patrol

Aircraft from dirigibles and landplanes to helicopters and flying boats have been used to search out and attack enemy submarines. Now, Lockheed has come up with a very interesting new idea for chasing subs, the *Large Sea Loiter Vehicle (LSLV)*. The *LSLV* is a flying boat with a double hull like a catamaran boat. It has four large turbofan engines mounted on top of the wings, which is high enough to keep them dry while riding in 20-foot (6-m) waves and from being damaged by salt water.

The *LSLV* will weigh 640,000 pounds (288,000 kg) at takeoff, including more than 55 tons (50 metric tonnes) of weapons and electronic equipment, and it should be able to fly more than 4,500 miles (7,200 km) before refueling. It would use *hydro-skis* (small wings that work under water) for quicker takeoffs and landings.

Lockheed's *Large Sea Loiter Vehicle (LSLV)*

# THE NEXT GENERATION

5

There are many clever ideas that could make airplanes of the future much better than any we have today, and they will certainly look a lot different, too. It is possible, however, that none of the designs described in this book will ever be built. What you have seen are artists' conceptions of airplanes that *could* be flying in 10 or 25 or 100 years. But even if these particular hypersonic transports, convertiplanes, and nuclear-powered flying wings are never built, some of the ideas may be used to design other, even better, aircraft. It takes better ideas to make better airplanes, and these designs show many of the best ideas that are being used to create the next generation of aircraft.

Across: Perhaps these "flying saucers" will be the airplanes of tomorrow.

# INDEX

The tail-first *VariEze* (above) and other home-builts have provided many good ideas for designers of future planes (see page 17).

**ACKNOWLEDGMENTS:** The photographs in this book are reproduced through the courtesy of: pp. 1, 34, 41, 44, 52, 55, 60, U.S. Air Force; pp. 2, 26, 30, McDonnell Douglas Corporation; pp. 5, 24 (top), 36, 37, 42, 43, 59, Lockheed Aircraft Corporation; p. 51, Northrop Corporation; pp. 6, 8, 10, 12, 14, 45, 47, Grumman Corporation; pp. 15, 32, 35, 38, Lockheed-California Company; pp. 16, 29, 64, Don Berliner; p. 18, Avtek Corporation; p. 19, Rhein-Flugzeugbau GmbH; p. 20, Experimental Aircraft Association; p. 22, Gates Learjet Corporation; p. 24 (bottom), Bell Helicopter Textron Company; pp. 25, 27, 28, 40, 53 (bottom), Boeing Aerospace Company; pp. 31, 33, 46, 49, NASA; p. 48, Dassault-Breguet; pp. 50, 53 (top), 54, Rockwell International Corporation; pp. 56, 58, Boeing Vertol Company; p. 57, Hughes Helicopters, Inc. Cover photographs courtesy of McDonnell-Douglas Corporation (front) and Dassault-Breguet (back).